# HERE COMES
# KATE

## Kay Chorao

Dutton Children's Books • New York

*For our own Katie*

CIP Data is available.

Published in the United States 2000 by Dutton Children's Books,
a division of Penguin Putnam Books for Young Readers
345 Hudson Street, New York, New York 10014
www.penguinputnam.com
Printed in Hong Kong    First Edition
ISBN 0-525-46443-3
3 5 7 9 10 8 6 4 2

# CONTENTS

# KATE'S SNOWMAN

Kate looked out the window.

"Snow, snow, snow,"

she sang.

"Today I will make

a snowman," said Kate.

"It will be round

like you, Mama,"

said Kate.

"And mean like you, George,"

said Kate.

"And big like you, Papa,"

said Kate.

"Have fun,"

said Mama and Papa.

Kate stood in the snow.

"Help," she cried.

"I can't move."

"Then sit," said George.

He rolled her in the snow.

"Whee," said Kate.

"Look, Mama.

Look, Papa.

I made a snowman,"

said Kate.

# KATE'S QUILT

At bedtime, Mama gave

Kate a surprise.

"What is it?" said Kate.

"Something soft and warm

for your bed," said Mama.

"Can I hug it?" asked Kate.

"It will hug you," said Mama.

"I know what it is," said Kate.

She opened the package.

"Oh," said Kate.

"It is a quilt.

I made it just for you,"

said Mama.

"I wanted a dolly."

Kate stamped her foot.

Mama looked sad.

"Good night, Kate," she said.

She closed the door

very quietly.

Kate pulled the quilt

off her bed.

She kicked it.

"I wanted a dolly,"

she cried.

She crawled under the sheet.

The bed was cold.

Outside, the trees

made scary shapes.

Kate pulled up the sheet.

It was too thin.

The scary tree shapes

could see her.

"Help!" cried Kate.

She jumped out of bed.

She grabbed the quilt.

She put it on her bed.

Then she crawled

under the quilt.

It was soft

and thick and warm.

It hugged her.

The scary tree shapes
couldn't see her.
Deep under her quilt,
Kate was warm and safe.

"Thank you, Mama,"

Kate said.

"You are very welcome,"

whispered Mama.

# KATE'S CAR

Kate wanted a car.

"Car," cried Kate.

"You are too small,"

said Mama.

"Car," cried Kate.

"You would crash,"

said George.

"Car," cried Kate.

"You would get lost,"

said Papa.

"Car," cried Kate.

"You might hurt someone,"

said Mama.

"Car," cried Kate.

She jumped up and down.

"She is bad," said George.

"Yes," said Papa.

"A little," said Mama.

Kate went out.

"Car," she cried.

"Here,"

said Rose.

"You left it at my house."

"Car," said Kate.

"Kate's car."

# KATE'S BOX

Cousin Otto was coming.

Kate hid in a box.

"Come out,"

said Mama.

"No," said Kate.

"I remember the last time

Otto came," said Kate.

Today Otto howled.

"Help Auntie change

his diapers," said Aunt Betty.

"No," said Kate.

"Waaa," howled Otto.

Papa left the room.

"Waaa," howled Otto.

Mama hugged him.

George tickled him.

Auntie kissed him.

"Waaa," howled Otto.

Everyone but Kate left.

"Too much noise,"

said Kate.

"ALL GONE,"

said Kate.

"Peekaboo!"